For Mrs Pea and our four little peas – K.P.

To my two little peas, Dara and Walter – A.W.

SIMON & SCHUSTER
First published in Great Britain in 2019 by Simon & Schuster UK Ltd
1st Floor, 222 Gray's Inn Road, London, WC1X 8HB
Text copyright © 2019 Kjartan Poskitt • Illustrations copyright © 2019 Alex Willmore
The right of Kjartan Poskitt and Alex Willmore to be identified as the author and illustrator
of this work has been asserted by them in accordance with the Copyright, Designs and
Patents Act, 1988 • All rights reserved, including the right of reproduction in whole
or in part in any form • A CIP catalogue record for this book is available
from the British Library upon request.
978-1-4711-7525-1 (PB) • 978-1-4711-7526-8 (eBook)
Printed in China • 10 9 8 7

THE RUNAWAY PEA

Kjartan Poskitt and Alex Willmore

SIMON & SCHUSTER
London   New York   Sydney   Toronto   New Delhi

It's six o'clock and we're ready for tea,
but look – what's that?

It's a RUNAWAY PEA!

He pinged off the plate with incredible force . . .

... then slipped and went

SPLAT

in a puddle of sauce.

The carrots and beans were all laughing with glee –
"You didn't get far, you piddling pea."

"Just watch!" said the pea.
"I've hardly begun.

I might only be small
but I want to have fun."

The pea shot away with a skip and a hop . . .

... then into the dog bowl he fell with a

PLOP!

Climb, little pea! Climb up the side –
QUICK, before Boris's mouth opens wide!

The runaway pea jumped amazingly high
and so nearly landed in Boris's eye!

He rolled along Boris's back in a flash,
but a flick of the tail sent him flying off . . .

"Get out of my tank!"
said Adele with a SQUIRT!

He fell on a mousetrap, which snapped with a **BANG**...

and bounced off a cobweb
that stretched and went

TWANG!

He came to a rest on a high, dusty shelf.
"So far, so good!" smiled the pea to himself.

"Surely there's nothing else
left to go wrong?"

Then a fan started up and it blew him along.

And what's that below with an orangey glow?
It's the slot in the top of the toaster . . .

OH NO!

In the pea fell, unable to stop,

then the toaster pinged up with an almighty

POP!

"OWWWW," cried the pea, "my bottom's on fire,"

as he flew straight on into the tumbling dryer.

Buffered

and battered

and bounced all about,

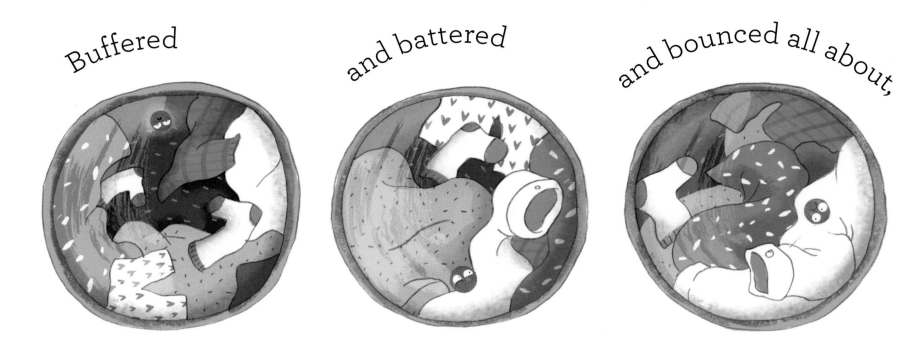

the pea was so glad when he finally got out.

He collapsed on a shirt that
had newly been washed . . .

LOOK OUT, little pea, or you're going to get squashed!

He tumbled and rolled along out of control . . .

... under the fridge to a dark, sticky hole.

PICK UP FOOD
FOR BORIS
SWEEP FLOOR
SWIMMING CLUB

Wash clothes
Send
Birthday
Card

MEGA-FRIDGE

Too weary to move, he just let out a groan ...
then got a strange feeling he wasn't alone!

Out of the gloom came mysterious shapes –
a dried-up banana and two mouldy grapes.
"Oh dear," said the pea. "What happened to you?"

"We were naughty," they said.
"We all ran away too.

We don't recommend it," they whimpered quite sadly.
"You'll get old and wrinkled and start to smell badly."

"I've changed my mind," said the runaway pea.
"I'll get back on that plate and be ready for tea."

"You won't," said the grapes,
"cos you've been on the floor.
Runaway pea, you're not
loved anymore."

The little pea trembled. He knew it was true.
There was nowhere to go for him, nothing to do.

Helpless and hopeless and feeling forlorn,
his tired eyes closed and he gave a big yawn.

But a magic thing happened while he was asleep . . .

. . . he woke up beside
the recycling heap.

The soil was soft and the weather was sunny,
and soon the pea started to feel a bit funny.

Under the ground he was sprouting some roots,
and out of his top he was shooting out shoots!

The shoots all had pods, and inside every one
was a party of new peas, all bursting with fun!

So if you should ever hear
POP, PING or SPLAT,

or a SPLOSH in the sink,
or a YOW from the cat,

or a RAPPERTY TAP in the cupboard, then please . . .

DON'T PANIC,

it's only those runaway peas!

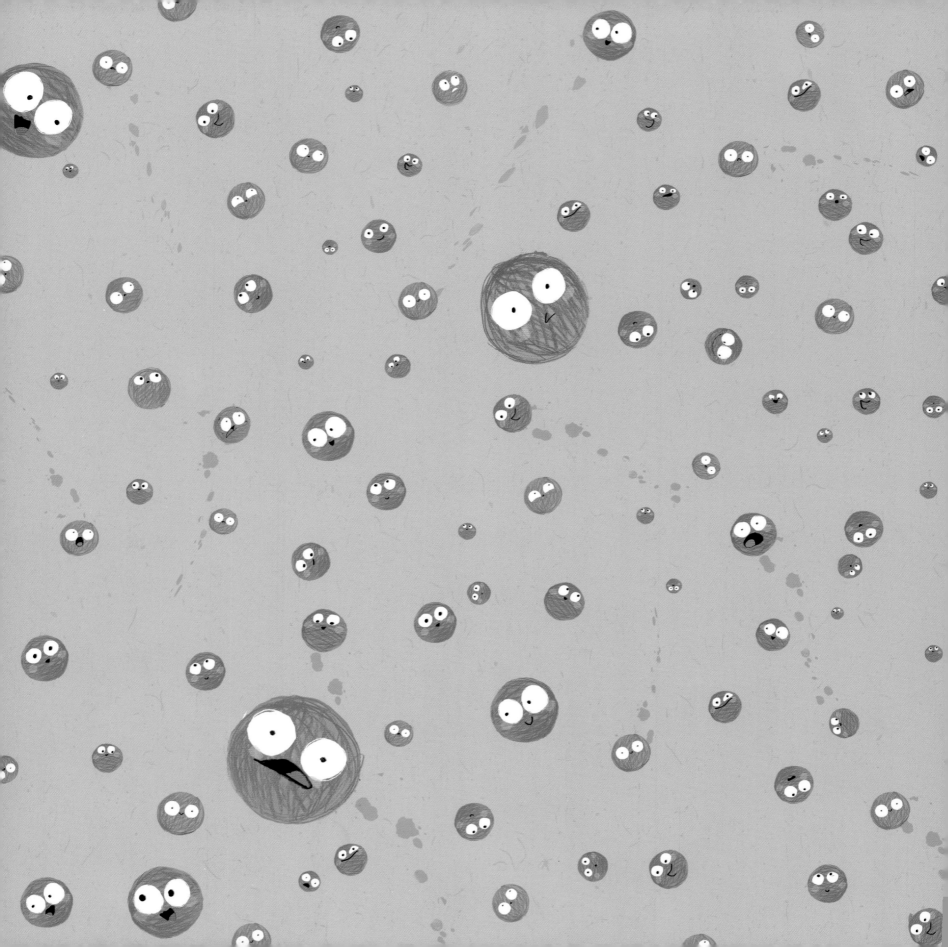

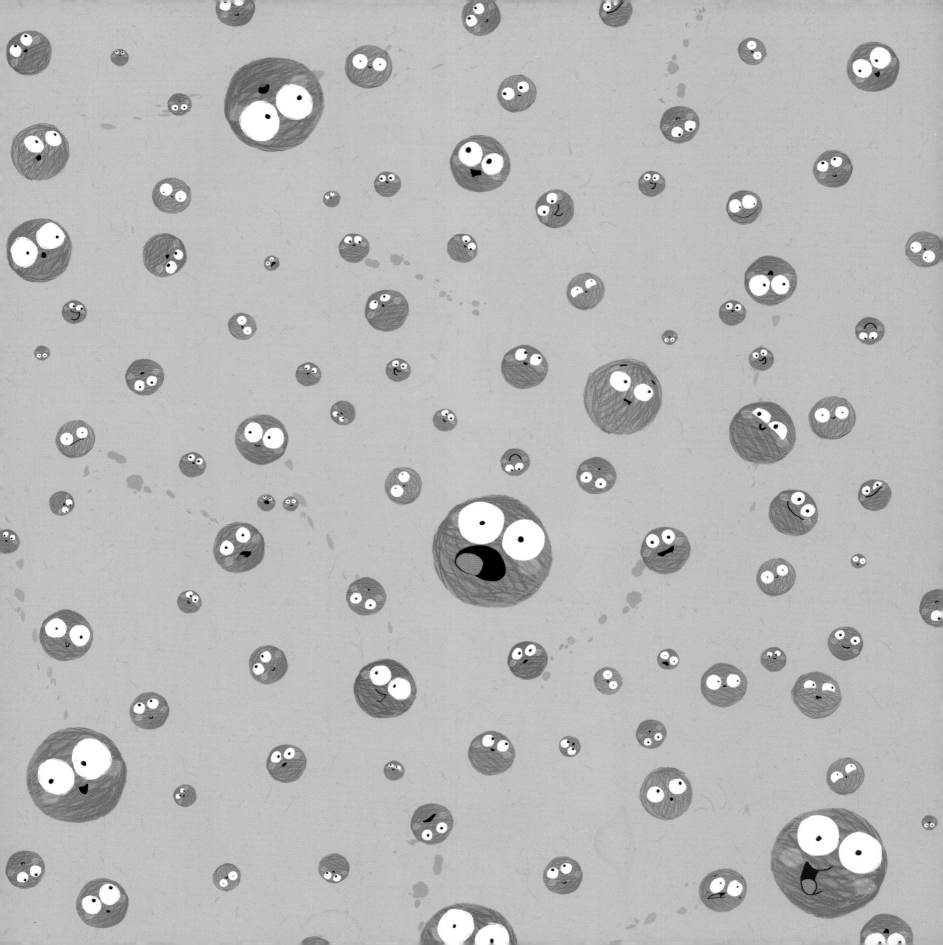

THE END

(No peas were harmed in the making of this book.)

BUS

Please renew or return items by due date

www.hertfordshire.gov.uk/libraries

Renewals and enquiries: 0300 123 4049

Textphone for hearing or
speech impaired users: 01992 555 506

**There's a lot going on at Hertfordshire
Libraries! Scan the QR code to find out
more . . .**

L32 06.23

Hertfordshire